Maisie
Hitchins

For Lucy, Sinead, Madeleine and Tabitha,
who told me how much they loved Maisie!
~HW

For Sylvie and Graham, with all my love
~ML

STRIPES PUBLISHING
An imprint of Little Tiger Press
1 The Coda Centre, 189 Munster Road,
London SW6 6AW

A paperback original
First published in Great Britain in 2013

Text copyright © Holly Webb, 2013
Illustrations copyright © Marion Lindsay, 2013

ISBN: 978-1-84715-382-1

The right of Holly Webb and Marion Lindsay to be
identified as the author and illustrator of this work
respectively has been asserted by them in accordance
with the Copyright, Designs and Patents Act, 1988.

A CIP catalogue record for this book is available from the British Library.

Printed and bound by CPI Group (UK) Ltd, Croydon, CR0 4YY.

2 4 6 8 10 9 7 5 3 1

Holly Webb Illustrated by Marion Lindsay

Maisie Hitchins

The Case of the Phantom Cat

Stripes

31 Albion Street, London

Attic:
Maisie's grandmother and Sally the maid

Third floor:
Miss Lane's rooms

Second floor:
Madame Lorimer's rooms

First floor:
Professor Tobin's rooms

Ground floor:
Entrance hall, sitting room and dining room

Basement:
Maisie's room, kitchen and yard entrance

Chapter One

Maisie dusted the Chinese vase on the hall table again. It wasn't in the slightest bit grubby any more, but she wanted an excuse to hang around above stairs, and she'd polished everything else she could find. She was waiting for her friend Alice to come for her French conversation lesson with Madame Lorimer, who lodged on the second floor.

The hall clock struck the quarter hour and she sighed. Alice clearly wasn't coming. Again. She had missed her lesson for the third week running now.

Maisie picked up her dusters and the beeswax polish and walked slowly down the back stairs to the kitchen, where Sally, the maid, was peeling potatoes at the big table. Maisie's grandmother was poking at a saucepan on the range, boiling a treacle sponge pudding for the lodgers' dinner.

The house at 31 Albion Street was divided up into apartments on the different floors and let out to lodgers. The best rooms on the first floor were let to Professor Tobin, who had filled them with glass cases full of strange stuffed animals and other odd relics he had collected on his travels. An actress, Miss Lottie Lane, lived on the third floor and

of course, Madame Lorimer, the French
teacher, was on the second.

"Goodness, have you only just finished?"
Gran frowned at Maisie.

Maisie crouched down to fuss over Eddie,
her dog. He had been asleep in his basket
close to the stove, but now he was leaping up
at her happily, his ears flapping. "Oh… Were
you waiting for Miss Alice again?" Gran said.

"She must be very ill," Maisie murmured worriedly as she stroked Eddie's silky ears. "It's more than a fortnight now since we've seen her."

"They sent a message to Madame Lorimer though, didn't they?" Gran asked, putting the lid back on the pan and patting at her steam-reddened face with her apron. "Did they not say what was wrong?"

"A putrid sore throat – that was all her governess said." Maisie glanced anxiously at Gran. "But it might have got worse. What if Alice has scarlet fever? George, the butcher's boy, told me that a little girl who lives on his street has it and she's very bad. The fever's spread all through the school."

George had been gorily dramatic about the scarlet fever when he'd delivered the meat that morning. He'd told Maisie that

Elizabeth, the little girl who lived a few houses down from his family, was bright red and bumpy all over. He said she looked like a strawberry. Although come to think of it, how did George know? He'd hardly have gone visiting. But at the time she'd been so fascinated by his description of Elizabeth the Strawberry that she hadn't thought to ask.

"And then her skin all started peeling off!" George had hissed.

It was like some dreadful ghost story, Maisie thought. "Is it catching?" she'd asked him.

"Catching! Of course it's catching!"
George had rolled his eyes at her. "Half the
school's got it. And there's nothing you can
do, you know." He'd shrugged. "Some
people get better. But most don't," he'd
added, biting his lip. "I just hope my little
sister's going to be all right. She was playing
hopscotch in the street with Elizabeth just a
few days ago. I don't want her going down
with the scarlatina."

Maisie had frowned. "Scarlatina?"
It sounded like some particularly nasty sort
of fairy. Perhaps one that went round
making people ill. Turning them into
strawberries with one flick of her wand.

"Same thing," George had explained
gloomily. "Just another name for it. Oh well.
Better get on."

Maisie looked wide-eyed at Gran,

imagining Alice with an awful scarlet rash.

Gran sniffed. "But Miss Alice doesn't go to school, does she? She has her own governess. So she would hardly have been mixing with those sort of children. And she's too old for scarlet fever, surely. Don't fuss, Maisie. The poor child probably just has a sore throat, like that governess of hers said."

Maisie smiled. "If Alice has any sense, she'll stay ill for as long as she can. I'd be ill, if I had to have lessons from a governess as horrible as Miss Sidebotham every day." But she was still playing with Eddie's ears, running them through her fingers and frowning. "Do you think I could go and visit her?"

"Did you dust everywhere upstairs?" Gran asked.

"Yes," Maisie sighed. She didn't enjoy housework, but she was good at it, because she'd had a great deal of practice. Even though they owned their own house and it was a tall one in a smart-ish London street, they certainly weren't rich and Gran needed Maisie's help.

Thirty-one Albion Street had a great many stairs and there was a lot of it to keep clean. Between Maisie and Gran and Sally, they managed it all and made a respectable living from the lodgers. But it had meant that Maisie had had to leave school well before she was twelve to help. Gran had told her that if anyone asked, she was to say that she had lessons from Madame Lorimer. There had been seventy children in Maisie's class at school, though, and Maisie reckoned her teacher had hardly noticed she was gone.

"Oh, go on then, Maisie. Go and see Miss Alice and find out how she is!"

"Can I really?" Maisie hugged her. "Oh, but Gran, they won't let me in to visit her looking like this, will they?" Maisie looked down at her faded wool dress and her apron. She was clean and neat, but certainly not smart. The servants at Alice's lovely house would know at once that she wasn't a suitable friend for a young lady.

"Go to the kitchen door, Maisie, for goodness' sake. All this detecting and you still haven't an ounce of common sense. Ask after Miss Alice and say Madame Lorimer sent you. Tell them you've a message for her, sending her good wishes, or something like that. And put your hat on!" Gran called, as Maisie dashed out of the kitchen. "Oh, and don't forget the dog! He's getting under my feet!"

Maisie tiptoed down the steps into the
basement and knocked quietly at the
kitchen door of Alice's house. She had never
been inside before – they usually met at
Maisie's or occasionally in the street when
Alice was out walking. But she was almost
always with a maid or her governess, which
meant they couldn't do much more than
smile and wave. Maisie had seen Miss
Sidebotham tell Alice off for even that.

"Now, be good," she whispered to Eddie
sternly. He had seen a cat on their way over
and Maisie hadn't managed to grab his
collar in time. He had barked madly and
chased it halfway down the street, nearly
tripping up several ladies out shopping. It
had taken her ages to catch him and it was
very embarrassing.

Eddie looked up at her innocently and

wagged his tail. Maisie sighed. He clearly
didn't feel guilty in the slightest.

Maisie was about to knock again when
the kitchen maid answered the door.
"Whatever do you want?" She stared at
Maisie in surprise then eyed
Eddie suspiciously.

Maisie smiled at her, trying not to look nervous. "I've come to bring a message for Miss Alice Lacey," she explained. "From Madame Lorimer, her French teacher. Madame wants to know how Miss Alice is."

"Oh…" The girl, who wasn't all that much older than Maisie, nodded. "I suppose you'd better come in then… Not him!" she added, in a genteel shriek, pointing at Eddie. "Cook would have my guts for garters. You'd better tie him up outside."

"I'll be back soon, I promise," Maisie whispered to Eddie, as she twisted the rope through the railings. "I should have put your diamond collar on – that would show her." Maisie and Eddie had tracked down an emerald and pearl necklace for a young actress and the actress's fiancé, who was a lord, had sent them both jewels as a reward.

Maisie was very proud of her bracelet and Eddie's collar, but they were a bit of a worry to wear. She kept them hanging on the wall of her room, instead, in a little glass case that Professor Tobin had given her.

"Who is it, Lizzie?" someone called and the maid bustled Maisie in.

"She's come calling for Miss Alice. From her French teacher," the maid said, pushing Maisie ahead of her, so that she ended up standing in front of a large newspaper. The owner of the newspaper was sitting at a scrubbed wooden table much like Gran's, except that it was in the middle of a kitchen about four times the size, with the very newest, smartest, shiniest kitchen range and shelves of huge tins and trays and china.

The person reached round her paper for the cup of tea that was next to her on the

table and then folded the paper up so she
could stare at Maisie. It was the cook.
"Would you be the young lady that Miss
Alice mentioned?" she asked. "Been working
at a theatre? Hunting for lost jewellery?"

"Yes." Maisie nodded, hoping that this wasn't going to get her thrown out. If the cook knew about the mysterious missing emerald, it could only be because Alice had told her. Perhaps she and Alice were friends. "Is Miss Alice any better?" she asked anxiously. "We only heard that she had a bad sore throat, but I haven't seen her for weeks."

The cook took a sip from her tea cup. "She's been confined to her room. They did think it might be diphtheria, but that was just the ninny of a governess making a fuss. Any news from upstairs this afternoon, Lizzie?" she said to the kitchen maid.

"Miss Alice said could she not have milk pudding for her supper again, but Miss Sidebotham said it was that or calves' foot jelly. So the upstairs maids told me, anyway. And after Miss Sidebotham had gone,

21

Miss Alice told Mary-Ann that if she brought her calves' foot jelly, she'd throw it in the fire."

Maisie giggled. "She sounds as though she's getting better then."

The cook nodded at her approvingly. "Did I hear Lizzie telling you to tie up a dog?"

"I did tie him up very carefully," Maisie promised. But she checked behind her just in case Eddie had slipped his collar and followed her.

"I'm sure you did, dear. But Miss Alice likes dogs. I always used to let her cut them out of gingerbread. Dogs and elephants. And I haven't an elephant on hand to cheer her up, so I reckon you and a dog might do. Lizzie, fetch me some of that gingerbread you made yesterday."

"But Miss Alice is only having milk pudding!" Lizzie protested.

"Stuff and nonsense. She'll waste away, poor child. Go and fetch your dog, Miss Whatever-your-name-is. Then you can leave your cape and hat here. And Lizzie, find Mary-Ann. You can't go sneaking upstairs."

When Maisie came back in with Eddie, who was wagging his tail madly at the delicious smells coming out of the range, there was another maid in the kitchen, wearing a smart black dress, a frilled apron and a pretty cap. But despite her smart outfit, she beamed at Maisie in a friendly sort of way and cooed over Eddie.

"Little sweetheart! He's bound to make Miss Alice feel better. Come on – I've found a laundry basket. Will he jump in it, if Miss Sidebotham comes spying around?"

Maisie nodded. "He'll stay if I tell him."
Which was *almost* always true.

Mary-Ann hurried Maisie up the back
stairs. "These go all the way to the first
floor," she explained, puffing as she lugged
the big wicker basket along. "There's a flight
of marble stairs down to the main hall, but
we don't use that. Ssshhh!" They were in a
beautifully carpeted passage now and
Maisie could hear someone coming –
someone with slow, heavy footsteps.

"The butler!" Mary-Ann whispered.
"He's a real stickler, likes everything perfect.
Put the little dog in the basket!"

Mary-Ann whipped the plate of
gingerbread out of the basket where she'd
been carrying it balanced on top of the
washing, and Maisie dropped Eddie in and
covered him in a sheet. Eddie poked his nose

out and peered at her, his ears twitching doubtfully, but when she put her finger to her lips and shushed him, he wriggled back underneath.

Just in time, Mary-Ann pushed Maisie behind a long velvet curtain. Maisie held her breath as the footsteps rounded the corner of the passage and came to a stop.

"What are you doing, girl?" a treacly voice inquired.

"Miss Sidebotham said she thought Miss Alice's pillowcases should be changed, sir. What with her having a temperature…"

"Hmm. Don't let the master of the house see you carrying baskets of washing about," he said.

"No, sir." Maisie could tell that Mary-Ann was trying not to giggle. She hoped it wasn't because the washing was wriggling too much.

"He's gone!" Mary-Ann whispered finally from around the curtain. "Come on! Hurry!"

Maisie grabbed Eddie out of the basket and followed the older girl down the hallway. They were going too quickly for her to take in much of the house, except that it seemed to sparkle. All the curtains were made of the same rich velvet as the one she'd been hiding behind and pictures glittered at her from gilded frames.

"This is Miss Alice's room." Mary-Ann knocked lightly and opened the door, holding it for Maisie and Eddie to walk in.

Maisie couldn't help gasping at the prettiness of Alice's room. The bed was draped with flowered curtains and there were two pink velvet chairs on either side of the fire. At one side of the room was the most enormous dolls' house, so big it needed a table all to itself.

"Maisie!" Alice had been lying down, just a small lump under the lace-covered bedspread, but she sat up, staring. She looked dreadful, Maisie thought, examining her anxiously. Her face was a palish yellow with dark shadows round her eyes and her pretty blonde hair had gone all stringy. But at least she wasn't in the slightest bit strawberry-looking.

"Now don't excite yourself, Miss!" Mary-Ann whispered. "Cook sent her up here, but we don't want you taking a turn for the worse. I'll stay outside and pretend to be dusting, then I can let you know if anyone comes. And Cook's sent you up some gingerbread, Miss." Mary-Ann took it out of the basket again and laid it on a little table, then she whisked out to guard the door.

"What happens if someone does come?" Alice asked, wide-eyed. Her voice was croaky, as though her throat still wasn't quite better.

"I'll hide under the bed," Maisie said. She checked beneath the frilly valance. "I could practically live under here!" Then she perched by Alice's feet and looked at her worriedly. "You don't look well. I did wonder whether you might have scarlet fever."

Alice shook her head. "No. Miss Sidebotham says it was all because I went for a walk when it was raining and didn't bother to change my stockings afterwards, but I think that's nonsense." She sighed. "I'm ever so sick of being ill. It's boring. It's so nice that you and Eddie have come."

"Haven't you had other visitors?" Maisie asked, as she put Eddie down on the bed.

"No – people probably thought it was scarlet fever and didn't want to risk it. But Papa visits me every day when he gets back from his office. He said he was going to have a surprise for me today – something I should really like. I tried to guess, but he wouldn't tell." Alice smiled at Maisie. "There you are, a chance to practise your detecting. You can tell me what the surprise is. Solve the mystery for me!"

Maisie pulled her magnifying glass out of her coat pocket and laid it on the silken bedcover. Then she found her notebook and pencil stub and stared at Alice, trying to put on a serious detective face. "Any clues?"

"No-ooo…" Alice shook her head. "He said I was sure to like it, that's all." She reached over to stroke Eddie. "Perhaps he's bought me a dog! Or a kitten…" She gave a little sigh. "Sorry, Eddie. But I would love a kitten. Oh, I hope Papa won't be held up at the office." She peered at the little gilt clock on the mantelpiece. "He should be here any minute, I think."

Maisie squeaked and jumped off the bed. "I'd better go then!"

Alice laughed. "Oh, don't! He'd like you."

The door suddenly flew open and Mary-Ann peered round the edge of it, flapping her hands at Maisie. "It's Mr Lacey! Hide!"

Maisie looked at the frilly valance round the bed, but Alice caught her hand. "Honestly. I've told him all about your adventures, Maisie. He won't be cross."

Footsteps sounded and a tall fair-haired man strode in and stopped in surprise when he saw Maisie and Eddie.

"Papa!" Alice called out croakily. "This is Maisie – the girl I told you about! She came to visit because I'd not been to my French lesson for so long and she was worried."

"That's very good of you." Mr Lacey gave Maisie a little half-bow. She bobbed her knees in a curtsey and started to sidle towards the door.

"Don't go, Maisie!" Alice pleaded.

Maisie looked across at Mr Lacey, who nodded, waving her towards one of the pink velvet chairs.

"Alice is right – please do stay. I haven't seen her looking this bright for a fortnight. She's even got colour in her cheeks." He smiled at her. "And I've some very good news for you, dearest Alice." Alice's father tugged thoughtfully at the end of his blond moustache.

Maisie watched him, wondering what it was he did at his office to make so much money. This was the largest, grandest house she had ever been in. It was even grander than the theatre she'd worked at, which had been quite shabby when you saw it without the gaslights and the excitement of the show.

It was difficult to detect someone who was sitting next to you, Maisie realized. She couldn't stare at Mr Lacey without being rude. She had to make do with quick glances. She thought he must smoke cigars, or perhaps a pipe – his moustache was stained brown at the ends. And his front teeth stuck out a little! A pipe, then, and he'd held it in his teeth so much it had pushed them out. Maisie felt quite proud of herself.

"So, shall I tell you about my surprise?" Mr Lacey asked, interrupting Maisie's thoughts.

"Oh, yes please! I've been wondering all day." Alice sat up further against her lace-edged pillows, watching him eagerly.

Her father beamed at her. "I've rented a house in the country for you to go to, my dear, so that you can breathe the fresh air and get properly well."

Alice's eyes widened. "Are you coming, too?" she asked hopefully.

"I wish I could," her father told her. "But I have to be at the office. Miss Sidebotham will go with you."

"Oh…" Alice sighed and drooped against her pillows.

Her father watched her anxiously and tugged his moustache again. "Unless… Unless you would like to go, too, Miss Maisie?"

Chapter Two

Maisie stared at him blankly. Even with all her careful detecting, she'd certainly never expected him to say that. "Me?" she gasped.

"Oh yes, yes, what a simply perfect plan!" Alice croaked. "Oh, Maisie, please say that you will."

"I'd have to ask Gran," Maisie murmured, but she was smiling hopefully to herself.

She had never been out of London – it would be an amazing adventure to travel to the country.

She could see why Mr Lacey wanted Alice to go. London this winter had been full of thick, choking fog. Sometimes it had been so bad that it was dark even at midday and if Maisie went out in it, the fog seemed to seep into her lungs so that she could taste it for the rest of the day. It seeped into the houses, too, under the doors and through the cracks in the windows, so it was impossible to escape. The thought of somewhere with trees and grass, which Maisie had only seen in the public parks, was wonderful.

Mr Lacey nodded. "Indeed, you must ask your grandmother." He patted Eddie's head, smiling. "And, of course, you'll take the little dog, too. You two would be the best sort of medicine for my dear girl, I should think. When Alice is feeling stronger, you could go out for walks with this little chap. Can you wait a little longer, Maisie? I will write a letter for you to take back to your grandmother now, with a proper invitation. And I shall promise that Miss Sidebotham will take the very best care of you."

Maisie rolled her eyes at Alice while Mr Lacey wasn't looking and Alice had to stuff the frilled sleeve of her nightgown into her mouth to stop herself laughing.

"If I come, I can help you stay out of her way," Maisie whispered.

Alice nodded hopefully. "It would be such fun!" she whispered back and she put out her thin little hand and held Maisie's tightly.

"But you've only just come back from that theatre!" Gran said, looking from the letter to Maisie and back again. "You're getting rather too much in demand, if you ask me." But she was smiling, so Maisie knew that she was joking.

Maisie sighed. "Don't worry, I'll tell them that I can't go. I can't leave you and Sally to do all the work again. Mr Lacey said that he had rented the house for a month."

Gran eyed her worriedly. "Having said that, there's ever such a lot of sickness about… You're rather old to catch scarlet fever, but even so, I wouldn't put it past you to come down with it, Maisie. And this fog isn't good for anyone. It would do you good to have a few weeks in the country, too."

"But how will you manage?" Maisie frowned at her.

Gran sniffed. "Well, there'll be a good deal less scrubbing of floors without that dog tracking mud all over them. He is invited, too, isn't he?" she added hopefully.

Maisie nodded. "Alice's father said that once she was a little better, we could take him out for country walks!"

Gran nodded. "And there's still some of the money left from your job at the theatre. If I have to, I can get someone in to help."

"So ... yes?" Maisie held her breath.

"Yes. If you promise me you won't get yourself mixed up in any more mysteries," Gran said. "Just try and behave like a young lady. Like that nice Miss Alice."

"Alice Honoria Lacey! Sit down this instant!" Miss Sidebotham said, in a sort of strangled shriek. She was far too concerned about manners to actually shout across the platform of Paddington Station, but Maisie could tell that she wanted to. Maisie sighed. They had only meant to walk down the platform to get a closer look at the engine, as she had never been on a train before.

Miss Sidebotham was clearly still furious about being saddled with Maisie as well as Alice. And she had been horrified that they were taking Eddie with them – *so* horrified that she kept on pretending that she just couldn't see him. Maisie could tell Eddie knew that the governess didn't like him.

He kept sitting down next to her and giving her long, soulful looks and then she would trip over him. Maisie couldn't work out if he was trying to win her over, or if he was just being annoying.

Miss Sidebotham had protested to Mr Lacey about them coming, or so Alice had told Maisie. Alice had overheard them talking about it. But her father had told Miss Sidebotham that he felt Alice needed another child with her for more interesting company. He said it was important that she was kept amused while she was recovering. Which obviously meant that he thought Miss Sidebotham was boring as well.

"Which is a great relief to me, Maisie," Alice had told her seriously, as they'd waited on the steps of the Laceys' grand house for the cab to take them to the station.

"Because Papa is a widower, of course, and one does hear of governesses marrying the master of the house really quite often. Imagine having Miss Sidebotham as a mother!"

"I don't want to," Maisie had said, shuddering.

"Exactly. But if he thinks she's a deathly bore as well, then he can't possibly want to marry her."

"He would be mad!" Maisie told Alice reassuringly, watching Miss Sidebotham snapping at the maids as they carried down the luggage. Her own things were in a rather embarrassingly small and battered leather suitcase that Gran had found in the attic. She could see it now in the pile of cases and boxes that was waiting to be put in the luggage van, next to Alice's smart dressing

case, with her initials embossed on it in gilt.
She did hope that the house they were going
to stay in wasn't too grand. Miss Sidebotham
was already giving her snooty looks all the
time. It would be horrible if the maids at
Wisteria Lodge despised her because she
didn't have six changes of clothes a day and
handmade lace on all of her petticoats.

"Is Wisteria Lodge very big?" she asked
Alice, as Miss Sidebotham shooed them back
across the platform to sit down.

"Quite big," Alice said thoughtfully. "Papa
showed me a drawing of it that the house
agent sent. It used to be a hunting lodge
that belonged to the Marquis of Walden, but
he only stayed there for a few weeks every
year. And then it was sold. It gets rented out
to people who want a country house to stay
in. Like us."

Maisie nodded. "What does Wisteria mean? Is it the name of the village near the house?"

Miss Sidebotham let out a genteel little snort and Maisie went pink.

"I had to ask Papa what it was," Alice said, glaring at her governess. "It's a climbing plant. Very pretty, he said – it has purple flowers. Wisteria Lodge is covered in it in the summer, but we'll only see the bare branches now, of course. The village is called Little Stoney and that's where the station is."

Maisie looked up at the huge clock hanging above her. "I think the train is due to leave in a few minutes. Look at those great clouds of steam. It's almost as foggy in here as it is out there! Do you think we'd better get on board?"

There were at least eight great engines snorting and bellowing out steam and the occasional spark. Maisie was glad that she had Alice with her – and Eddie, although *he* wasn't much comfort. He didn't like the steam engines either and he kept having to bark at everything to make himself feel better. A well-bred and snobbish spaniel was also waiting to get aboard the train and it was giving him the most despising looks.

"Come along, Alice. And you," Miss Sidebotham added with a sigh, as though she would quite like to leave Maisie on the platform. "They've loaded our baggage now, so we must find the compartment your father reserved." She hurried them down the platform into a first-class carriage.

Maisie could hear her muttering that the mongrel should surely be travelling in the guard's van. She picked Eddie up, determined not to let anyone take him away from her.

"Don't let him on the seats!" Miss Sidebotham snapped, as Eddie went sniffing around the compartment.

"He wouldn't!" Maisie protested. "He knows he's not allowed on furniture."

"He's a very well-behaved little dog," Alice added. It was unfortunate that the spaniel trotted along the corridor just then and Eddie barked so loudly that the spaniel's grand lady owner asked her maid for smelling salts.

"We should not have brought that … creature!" Miss Sidebotham hissed. "He is not fit for polite society."

"He'll be good, Miss, I promise," Maisie said breathlessly, catching Eddie and trying to persuade him to curl up nicely under the seat. "I brought him a bone and a blanket to sleep on. He'll be quiet." She rummaged around in the rush basket Gran had given her for odds and ends, and pulled out the bone – George, her friend from the butcher's shop, had given it to her and it was almost as big as Eddie himself. She reckoned it would last for most of the journey.

The governess collapsed on to the opposite seat with her handkerchief pressed over her face, which Maisie thought was just rudeness. The bone hardly smelled at all.

"Little Stoney! Little Stoney!" The station master was striding up and down the platform with his flag, roaring like a foghorn.

"Do hurry, girls! Have you got all your things, Alice? The travelling chess set? Your *Latin Grammar*?"

"Yes, Miss Sidebotham. We really should get off the train now, Miss Sidebotham – the station master is looking most impatient."

The girls tumbled off the train with Eddie dancing excitedly round them. Maisie looked around at the tiny village station. She hadn't really known what to expect – it wasn't a bit like the huge London terminus. Just one short platform, a little ticket office and a cottage that had to belong to the station master. Miss Sidebotham stood on the platform, counting all the cases. A young boy came over to take them out into the road to be loaded on to a wagon and she fussed around him.

"We're just going to stretch our legs," Alice called, pulling Maisie and Eddie after her out on to the road and ignoring Miss Sidebotham's worried squeaks.

They stood watching the boy handing the cases up on to the wagon and Maisie noticed gladly that her suitcase really was there. She wouldn't have put it past Miss Sidebotham to leave it behind on purpose.

"So you're the young ladies going to Wisteria Lodge, then?" the boy asked curiously.

Alice went pink and Maisie nodded. "Yes. Is it far from here?"

"No, only a mile or so. But rather you than me."

"What do you mean?" Maisie asked, frowning. "Isn't it a nice house?"

He shrugged. "It's big. But I wouldn't call it nice. It's haunted for a start."

"Haunted?" Alice gasped and grabbed Maisie's arm.

Maisie snorted. "No, it isn't," she said. "You're just trying to scare us. You don't actually believe in ghosts, do you?"

The boy stopped loading cases and folded his arms, gazing at Maisie and Alice. "The last two – no, three families that took the house have stayed less than a year. Less than a month, the last lot. Strange noises. Odd white shapes in the passageways. The last family went to the vicar and asked him if Wisteria Lodge had been built over a plague pit!"

"What's a plague pit?" Alice whispered. She'd gone horribly white again so Maisie slipped an arm around her.

"It's a grave for people who died of the plague," Maisie explained. "But I'm sure the house isn't built anywhere near one. Who'd build a house on top of something like that? I bet the vicar told them that. Didn't he?"

"Yes…" the boy admitted. "He said it was stuff and nonsense. But they still left!" he added triumphantly. "They said the ghosts definitely smelled like a plague pit!"

"What on earth are you girls doing?" Miss Sidebotham appeared behind them, looking down her nose at the boy. Somehow she managed to make it obvious that she thought it was all Maisie's fault they had fallen into bad company.

"Oh, Miss Sidebotham, this boy says Wisteria Lodge is haunted!" Alice told her in a trembly voice.

"What nonsense," the governess said, but she sounded almost as trembly as Alice.

Maisie rolled her eyes at the boy, who was smirking, obviously very pleased with the success of his story. She squeezed Alice's hand and tried to sound confident. "What a lot of hogwash – there aren't any such things as ghosts!"

Chapter Three

"It *looks* haunted…" Alice said faintly, as the hired carriage drew up outside Wisteria Lodge.

Maisie peered out of the window. The house didn't look haunted to her. Scarily large and grand, but that was all. It did have a rather neglected air though – there were a few weeds growing in the drive and the windows could have done with a good clean.

A smartly dressed maid opened the door and Maisie could see a huge chandelier hanging in the entrance hall. She was far more worried about forgetting her manners in such a huge place than she was about any ghosts.

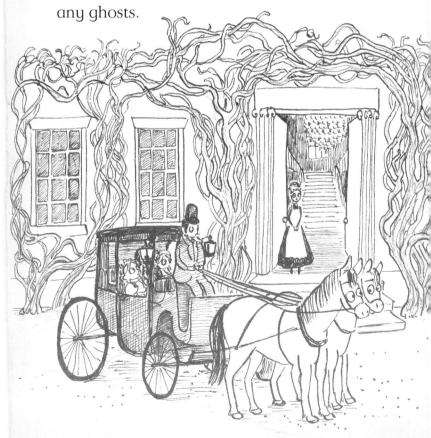

"There really isn't any such thing as ghosts," she said comfortingly to Alice. "That boy was just trying to scare us. Boys do that. George does it to me all the time."

"Who is George?" Miss Sidebotham demanded in a shocked voice.

"The butcher's boy, Miss," Maisie replied.

"Humph." Miss Sidebotham got down from the carriage and looked over at the house. "Well, it will do, I suppose. I am Miss Sidebotham, Miss Lacey's governess," she said to the maid, her nose in the air as she pranced up the marble steps. "Our luggage is following. We will wait in the drawing room, where we shall require tea." She marched off down the hall, opening doors as she went.

The maid looked surprised and slightly annoyed by the governess's hoity-toity manner, but she smiled at Maisie and Alice as they got down from the carriage.

"Hello!" Maisie smiled back. "This is Miss Alice and I'm Maisie. I've come to keep her company."

"And I'm Annie, Miss," the maid told her. "The parlourmaid. So you're the poor dear who's been ill?" she said sympathetically to Alice. "Mrs James – that's the cook – she's planned some lovely meals to fatten you up again, Miss Alice."

Alice beamed at her. "That sounds wonderful. At home they kept trying to make me eat calves' foot jelly and I hate it."

"Have you worked here for a long time?" Maisie asked curiously, as the maid led them into the house and shut the huge front door. The entrance hall made Maisie feel shabby – the marble staircase shone, even on such a grey day, and the chandelier glittered.

There were delicate chairs dotted about – chairs that looked too fragile even for Alice to sit on – and dark, ancient-looking paintings. "Did you work for the marquis who used to own the house?" She was wondering if Annie knew about the ghost stories.

"Goodness no, Miss. It's been empty for ages, this house. Me and Mrs James and Cissie and Lily, the other maids, we've all just come up from the village, only a couple of days before you. We've been up all hours, trying to get the old place ready. It's meant a lot of work, since the house has been empty so long. Some of the rooms are still under dust sheets, but Mr Lawrence, the house agent, he said you might not need them all, being as there's only the three of you."

Alice giggled. "How many bedrooms are there?"

"I lost count, Miss," Annie told her. "We've got the nicest ones ready, though. Must be at least fifteen of them altogether, I'd say."

Maisie looked at Alice. "Ooh, I don't know. I think I need at least fifteen bedrooms."

"And a couple of parlours and a breakfast

room," Alice added firmly.

"We're teasing," Maisie told Annie hurriedly when she saw a worried expression flit across her face.

"We made the lilac parlour ready for you, Miss, and the drawing room and the dining room, but the breakfast room's still all shut up…"

"You must have worked terribly hard," Alice said seriously. "We are grateful."

"Even if Miss Sidebotham looks like a mouse died under her nose," Maisie added. "Don't worry. She's always like that." She eyed Annie sideways. "The boy loading the luggage said that the last people here didn't stay very long. Did you work for them, too?"

Annie shook her head. "No, in the past people have always brought their own servants with them."

"Oh…" Maisie hesitated, but Alice elbowed her in the ribs.

"Ask her!"

"The boy said Wisteria Lodge was haunted…" Maisie said. "Is it?" She crossed her fingers under her jacket. She didn't want Alice even more worried. "It must be just a story, surely."

Annie looked round to see if anyone else was listening – perhaps she thought Miss Sidebotham would disapprove of her gossiping with the girls, which was almost certainly true. Maisie glanced over her shoulder to make sure the governess was still safely in the drawing room.

"The last two lots of lodgers certainly did leave in a tearing hurry, Miss! Last time it was a lady and a gentleman and they left in the middle of the night – their carriage went galloping through the village as though the hounds of hell was after them!"

"Oh, Maisie," Alice moaned. "It's true!"

"Of course it isn't! Look at this lovely house," Maisie said bravely. "How could it be haunted? It's so beautiful."

But she couldn't help glancing behind her as Annie showed them into the drawing room. The entrance hall was beautiful, but it was full of dark pools of shadow, where the strangest things could be lurking…

The delicious lemon cake and the scones that Mrs James had sent up for tea almost cured Alice of her ghost worries, but not quite. She was still nervous in the big house and she didn't like walking down the passages without Maisie.

Luckily, the two girls had bedrooms next to each other, with a little door that opened between the two. Maisie was fairly sure that her bedroom was about the size of the whole basement floor of her house at 31 Albion Street. And the huge four-poster bed was bigger than her entire bedroom.

"Goodnight, Maisie!" Alice called sleepily from the next room. They had decided to keep the little door open so that they could talk to each other, but they were just too tired to chat.

"Goodnight!" Maisie called back.

Eddie whined and yawned and curled himself into a tiny ball on the old blanket. Annie had found a basket for him in the kitchens, but Maisie was hoping Eddie might decide to sleep on the end of the bed. Her toes were quite chilly.

It was darkest night when Maisie woke up a few hours later and at first she couldn't remember where she was. Even in the darkness she could tell she wasn't in her cramped little room at home – the air smelled different. And there was a strange noise, not the watchman calling the hours, or a cab-horse trotting home. A wailing noise…

Maisie clutched the blankets round her and wriggled up a little, suddenly remembering that she was in a haunted house.

"There's no such thing as ghosts," she whispered fiercely to herself. Saying it out loud made her feel more certain somehow. She reached out for the box of matches and her hand shook a little as she lit her bedroom candle. She held it up, nodding as she ticked off a list of things that should be there – Eddie in his basket, the huge mahogany wardrobe where she'd hung her few dresses, the darker shape that was the open doorway to Alice's room.

The wailing noise came again, followed by a horrified gasp from the room next door.

"Maisie!" Alice sobbed. "A ghost!"

And through the door came a small white shape, wispy and thin. A little white ghost cat, that padded across the room and disappeared.

Chapter Four

Eddie woke up, snuffling and whining, and then let out a sharp, surprised bark. He jumped out of his basket and pattered across the room to Maisie, with his tail held tightly against his legs.

Maisie stared at him, her heart thumping. A ghost cat! She had seen a ghost cat! And Eddie had seen it, too! Then there was a whispering noise and a little thud and she shrank back against the pillows, wondering what was going to run through her room next.

A white, fluttery shape appeared in the doorway. Maisie had actually opened her mouth to scream before she realized it was only Alice – Alice in her lace-trimmed white nightgown. Alice, who was even more scared than she was.

"Did you see it?" she whispered, her teeth chattering.

"Yes. Look, get in with me, you'll freeze." Maisie beckoned her over to the bed and Alice scuttled towards her.

"That was a ghost!"

"Yee-eesss. Maybe." Maisie wasn't quite so sure now. After all, a moment ago, she would have sworn Alice was a ghost, too. And who'd ever heard of a phantom cat?

"Maisie, how can you doubt it?" Alice gasped. "The boy was right – and Annie. We both saw it. A real ghost! We must go back to London tomorrow morning. I can't stay here with a ghost!"

Maisie looked at her thoughtfully. "It was only a cat, though. I thought you liked cats."

"Not spectral ones!" Alice shuddered.

"I know it was scary," Maisie murmured,

"but it didn't seem to be a mean ghost… If it *was* one, which I still don't believe it was."

"What else could it have been, though?" Alice squeaked indignantly. She sat up and glared at Maisie. "We didn't imagine it!"

"I know… And Eddie saw it, too." Maisie sighed. "But I don't want to go back to London. Think of all that horrible fog. You won't get better – or not as fast, anyway."

"I think I'd rather be ill than haunted," Alice said, but she sounded uncertain. "Papa was so pleased that he'd found this house for us. He told me before we left that he'd been very worried about me staying in London." She sighed. "You're right, Maisie. We can't go back. Not just because of one little ghost cat, anyway." She gripped Maisie's wrist. "But if a skeleton walks through my bedroom clanking with chains,

Maisie Hitchins, or anything carrying its head under its arm, we're going home that very minute, do you hear? Even if we have to freeze on the station platform all night waiting for a train!"

"Lessons! You can't mean it, Miss Sidebotham!" Alice protested. "I'm ill." She coughed pathetically to prove it, but Maisie had seen the size of the breakfast she had eaten and the governess had, too.

"Perhaps not a full morning of lessons then," Miss Sidebotham agreed. "Since you are still recovering. But you can't be allowed to forget all that you've learned, Alice."

"And what's Maisie to do while I'm doing arithmetic and sewing?" Alice asked.

Miss Sidebotham sniffed. "Perhaps she

could help the maids. The house is under-staffed."

Maisie looked down at her plate, embarrassed. It was true that she would usually be doing the sort of things that Annie and Cissie and Lily were doing. She had felt very strange sitting about being waited on. But Miss Sidebotham didn't have to say it in that nasty sort of voice.

"Maisie is a guest! Papa invited her!" Alice snapped indignantly.

Miss Sidebotham gave another of those meaningful sniffs. This one clearly said that Mr Lacey had been very much misguided.

Maisie twisted her napkin in her fingers and comforted herself that at least she didn't have a name that sounded exactly like Side Bottom. And the bottom to match, even with a corset that was laced so tight it creaked. The governess was lucky that Alice was far too well behaved to tease her about it. "I can help the maids, Alice," she said quietly. "I could dust our rooms, at least."

"Good." Miss Sidebotham nodded triumphantly. Then she patted the frills at the front of her dress and frowned. "My spectacles! Now, where on earth are they? Have either of you girls seen them?"

Alice shook her head and looked gloomily into what was left of her porridge.

Maisie frowned thoughtfully. Miss Sidebotham usually wore her little gold pince-nez spectacles on a fussy gold chain, so that they hung round her neck when they weren't perched on the end of her nose.

"I haven't seen them, Miss Sidebotham," she said, shaking her head. "Not since yesterday, I'm sure."

"I must have left them in my room. Alice, I have left your books on the table in the lilac parlour, where we shall have our lessons. Go and cast an eye over your Latin vocabulary, while I find my spectacles."

Maisie was in the hallway with Eddie, admiring the chandelier and thinking about going down to the kitchens to ask for a duster and some furniture polish, when Miss

Sidebotham came hurrying down the marble staircase.

"Maisie! When did you say you saw my spectacles?" she snapped.

"You were wearing them when we had dinner, Miss," Maisie told her. "You couldn't find them upstairs?"

"No! Someone has taken them! That gold chain was a present from one of my previous employers and it is most valuable. I *know* I left the spectacles in the china tray on the dressing table in my room. Someone must have stolen them!" Miss Sidebotham was scarlet with rage and practically shouting.

Alice popped her head out of the lilac parlour. Maisie wondered if the maids could hear from down in the kitchens.

"It must have been that insolent girl who answered the door to us yesterday. She lit the fire in my bedroom this morning and she woke me, quite deliberately, clattering the fire irons about."

"If she were going to steal your gold chain, Miss, she wouldn't want to wake you," Maisie pointed out. "She'd want you to stay asleep in case you saw her take the chain."

"Don't be so impertinent!" Miss Sidebotham snapped. "Of course it was her. Unless *you* took them *yourself*, which wouldn't surprise me in the least."

Maisie gaped at her, shocked. She had never been accused of stealing before and she didn't know what to say.

"Maisie isn't a thief!" Alice cried, running out into the hallway. "She's a detective!"

"Nonsense." Miss Sidebotham looked crosser than ever and when Annie came into the hallway from the kitchens, the governess glared at her.

"Is anything wrong, Miss?" Annie asked. "We heard a-a disturbance."

"Did you indeed?" Miss Sidebotham sniffed again. "Yes, there most certainly is something wrong. My spectacles – and the gold chain attached to them – have disappeared."

"Oh dear, Miss." Annie frowned. "Could they have fallen off your dressing table?"

"So you knew that's where I had put them?" Miss Sidebotham snapped.

"Well, yes, Miss. I saw them when I came in to light your bedroom fire this morning. The dressing table's by the window, you see. If you remember, you asked me last night to open the window for you in the morning. Quite determined about it, you were."

"Fresh air is most important," Miss Sidebotham said, nodding.

"That's as may be, Miss, but that window stuck something dreadful. Not been opened in years, I'd say. So I was rattling away at it, right next to the dressing table. Of course I saw your spectacles."

"Hmmm." Miss Sidebotham still sounded suspicious and Annie frowned back at her.

"Why, Miss? You're not suggesting I took them, are you?"

The governess folded her arms and looked down her nose at Annie – which was quite difficult, as she was considerably shorter than the maid. "You are the only person who has been in my room."

"Well!" Annie folded her arms, too, and glared so furiously that Miss Sidebotham stepped back, nearly falling over Eddie. "I never heard the like. Calling me a thief! I'm not staying here to be treated like this." She started to undo the ties at the back of her apron, as if she intended to throw it on the floor and march out of the house there and then.

"Please don't go, Annie." Alice hurried forward. "Miss Sidebotham, I'm sure we'll find your spectacles. It must be a mistake. They must have fallen down the back of the dressing table or something." She ushered her governess over to one of the little chairs, murmuring, "Don't worry". Then she came over to Maisie and Annie and added in a whisper, "I don't suppose Eddie…?"

Maisie looked down at the little dog, who stared back at her, with one paw held up and his ears quivering, as though Miss Sidebotham had dealt him a death-blow. She shook her head. "He hasn't been in her room, I'm sure of it. I bet she's lost them herself."

Annie pulled a handkerchief out of the pocket of her apron and dabbed at her eyes, although Maisie couldn't see if she was actually crying. "Such a shock… To be called a thief like that. I'm not sure I can stay here to be insulted…"

Maisie patted her arm comfortingly. "It's just a misunderstanding, Annie, that's all." She glanced at Alice. If Miss Sidebotham upset Annie again, she was clearly going to flounce off and leave, which would make it even more difficult for the other maids to look after this huge house. Maisie didn't mind helping out, but the whole point of her being here was to keep Alice company. She could do dusting at home.

"I hope so," Annie said tearfully. "It's bad enough as it is, with all these strange goings-on."

"What strange goings-on?" Alice asked in a horrified voice.

"That's what I was coming to tell you, Miss. Cissie and Lily say there's a dreadful smell coming from the library. They went to take off the dust sheets and air it out, seeing as your governess said that you'd want to use it."

"Do we?" Alice asked, looking at Miss Sidebotham in surprise.

"For your lessons, Alice! It will be most useful," the governess said. "It can't be that

hard to take off the covers and light a fire!
I am going upstairs to keep looking for my
spectacles." She swept away crossly and
Maisie sighed, exchanging an understanding
look with Annie.

"It isn't just the smell, Miss…" Annie said,
in a doom-laden voice. "Noxious vapours,
they say there was. Like a green fog. And
then a terrible screeching noise, echoing
about the room. The two of them came
running back down to the kitchens shrieking
as though they were being murdered." She
looked around at them smugly, enjoying her
audience. "And they say they won't go back
in there even for double wages," she added
in triumph.

"Where is the library?" Maisie asked. She
still wasn't sure where half the rooms were.

"Over on that side of the hall, Miss. Down

the passage," Annie explained. "There's a couple of small parlours and the billiard room down there, too. It's all been shut up, though."

"Let's go and see," Maisie said, picking up Eddie for moral support and marching off down the passage with Alice and Annie following after her.

"Do we have to?" Alice whispered, as they padded along – the corridor was quite dark, as all the windows had shutters over them, and portraits loomed out of the shadows in a most nerve-racking way.

"It's probably just a dead mouse," Maisie pointed out. "We had one once, behind a wardrobe in Madame Lorimer's rooms – it stunk the place out."

"That wouldn't explain the noxious vapours, though." Annie shook her head.

"Rising out of the floorboards, Cissie said they were."

Alice gasped, but Maisie gave Annie a doubtful look. "Are you sure?"

"Well, I didn't see them myself, of course," Annie admitted. "But there was the screeching as well, don't forget. There's something unearthly in that room, Miss. Or under it…"

"What's that supposed to mean?" Maisie demanded, as they reached the library door. A pile of cleaning things lay abandoned just outside, where the maids had left them as they'd run away, and even though Maisie was trying hard not to believe in ghosts, the gaping doorway made her shudder.

"This house is haunted, Miss, I'm certain of it," Annie said, as they peered cautiously round the door. The library looked perfectly

normal now – only as spooky as any dimly-
lit room with the furniture covered in dust
sheets. "There, can't you smell it?"

Maisie and Alice sniffed and Alice started to cough horribly. "Oh, that's disgusting. Maisie, that can't just be a dead mouse."

"A rat maybe…" Maisie muttered. It really was a dreadful smell – so bad it felt like she could see it, seeping out of the floor and coating the back of her throat.

"It's the dead, Miss…" Annie moaned dramatically. "Rising up out of their graves!"

Chapter Five

Maisie and Alice had decided most definitely
that they did not need to use the library.

"Imagine sitting in there!" Alice whispered
to Maisie, as they helped Annie carry the
dusters and sweeping brush back along the
passage and down to the kitchens. "You'd
always be wondering what it was creeping
up behind your chair and putting its cold

fingers on your neck…"

"Oh, don't, Miss!" Annie moaned. "This house is built on a graveyard, everyone says so…"

Maisie sighed. Annie was a born gossip, she thought. And she was doing a very good job of frightening Alice to death.

"I still think it was a dead rat," she said firmly.

"Maybe it's a ghost rat now, like the ghost cat we saw!" Alice said suddenly, dropping the dustpan so it clattered down the kitchen stairs, and staring at Maisie in horror.

"You actually saw a ghost, Miss?" Annie gasped and the two other maids came out of the kitchen, looking terrified.

"She saw it?"

"Ooohhh, I can't stay here! Not with all those dreadful shrieking noises…"

The youngest of the maids was in tears and she was actually shaking. "They made my skin creep, Miss, and now you've seen a real ghost! I can't stay here, I just can't."

The cook, a tiny lady in a print dress and an apron all covered in flour, came hurrying out after them. "What? You've seen it?"

"It was just a little white cat—" Maisie started to say, but no one was listening to her. Mrs James was having the vapours and being held up by Annie and one of the other maids. The youngest maid, Lily, was kneeling on the floor and calling on the soul of her dead grandmother to save her from this evil house.

Even Alice looked slightly surprised by the scene she'd set off. "Please don't cry," she murmured to Mrs James, but it was no good.

"I can't stay here to be murdered in my bed by ghosts!" the cook gasped. "No one said anything about hauntings when I took the job! I'm leaving – now!"

"And me!" both Lily and Cissie chimed in and Annie nodded grimly, "Me, too."

"But you can't!" Maisie gasped. "You've had wages in advance. And you have to give notice, surely, so we can find someone else?"

"You won't. No one's going to want to work here," Annie pointed out. "Not when we tell them what it's like. And ghosts weren't mentioned when we were engaged, like Mrs James said. False pretences, that is. I'm going to pack." And she marched away up the stairs, with the others following after her.

"This is ridiculous…" Maisie muttered. "I don't believe this house is haunted at all. The boy at the station said the last people asked the vicar about a plague pit and he told them it was nonsense."

"But the cat…" Alice reminded her. "I suppose the smell could just be a dead rat. But we both saw the cat and so did Eddie. Perhaps we should write to Papa and ask him to fetch us home?"

"Well, we haven't come across a skeleton yet," Maisie reminded her.

"I suppose so…" Alice agreed reluctantly. "But what are we going to do without any servants?"

Maisie frowned. "Have you ever done any cooking?"

Alice shook her head. "No. Well, only gingerbread elephants. I'm allowed to sit on the edge of the kitchen table and watch our cook." She giggled. "She lets me hide from Miss Sidebotham sometimes."

"We might need a bit more than gingerbread…" Maisie said. "I wonder where Miss Sidebotham is. I'd have thought she'd have come searching for you by now. Maybe she's still hunting for her spectacles."

Maisie tiptoed into the kitchen and peered at the pans bubbling on the stove. "Well, it looks like we'll get our lunch, at least," she said. "I know how to use a stove like this, I think. It isn't all that different from the one my gran has. Just bigger." She wandered around the kitchen, looking at the boards full of chopped vegetables and the mound of washing up piled in the scullery next door. "I suppose at least there's only the three of us now," she said thoughtfully. "Mrs James was having to cook for seven. And all the food must be delivered from the shops in the village. I should think there's enough in here for the rest of the week," she added, peeping into the huge stone-floored larder. "Look at all that cheese! And there's a side of bacon, eggs, everything!"

"Maisie, do you actually think we can cook for ourselves?" Alice asked doubtfully.

"I can't make calves' foot jelly..." Maisie told her apologetically.

Alice smiled. "Thank goodness."

"It won't be the sort of thing Mrs Daley serves you at home, or like that delicious dinner Mrs James sent upstairs yesterday. No French cuisine, no Sweetbreads à la Maître d'Hôtel."

Alice shuddered. "I don't mind. Sweetbreads aren't what they sound like at all. Can we do this washing up? It looks quite fun."

Maisie looked at the pile and sighed. "I think I'd better wash. Miss Sidebotham would have forty fits if you reddened your hands. There's some boiling water in the copper – it's still steaming hot. You can dry. I saw aprons somewhere. Oh, here look." She pulled two out of a drawer in the dresser and they put them on. Alice was giggling as though it was an adventure and Maisie

couldn't help laughing, too. It was hard to
imagine someone who had never washed
up in their life. She watched Alice anxiously
as she handed her the pretty china teacups,
but Alice was actually far more careful than
she was.

"My gran would say you're a good worker," she told Alice approvingly and her friend went pink with pleasure.

"Do you think Miss Sidebotham will be cross?" she asked, as she dried another plate.

Maisie shrugged. "She doesn't have much choice, does she? Not if she wants to eat. But once she knows the servants have gone, I should think she'll write to your father. Or maybe even telegraph him. And I doubt if she'll be much use in the kitchen."

Alice sighed. "I suppose so."

"Girls! Girls! Alice, where are you?" A thin, frightened voice echoed down from the main part of the house – it was Miss Sidebotham. Maisie and Alice exchanged looks and hurried through the servants' quarters, pulling off the aprons as they went.

"What is it?" Alice asked anxiously, as they

found Miss Sidebotham tottering down the last steps of the marble staircase. She was horribly pale and she had her handkerchief pressed against her lips as though she felt sick. "You still can't find your spectacles?"

"Spectacles…" the governess whimpered. "I have just seen a spectre!" And she fainted to the floor.

Miss Sidebotham was laid out on the drawing room sofa with her handkerchief, smelling salts and a little brass bell she had found on the mantelpiece. She kept ringing it to call Alice and Maisie to bring her cups of tea and anchovy paste sandwiches, both of which, luckily, were quite easy to make.

It was a phantom cat that she had seen, she had explained, when she was well enough to talk. Apparently it had flitted down the upstairs corridor, outside her room, and frightened her into a fit. When the girls told her that the servants had walked out, she went into what she called a nervous collapse.

"I thought ghosts only came out at night," Maisie said to Alice, as she cut bread for sandwiches and fed the trimmed crusts to

Eddie. Miss Sidebotham liked them like that – she was very particular about her sandwiches, they'd found.

"I hadn't thought of that," Alice said, frowning as she stirred the tea in the pot. "Perhaps the cat is ever such a powerful ghost… Oh drat! That's Miss Sidebotham's bell again!"

"Well, she'll just have to wait! Honestly, she's your governess and she's got you running around after her like a slave. You're supposed to be resting."

Alice nodded. "I know. But I do feel so much better already, away from that dreadful fog. And this is fun."

The bell jangled again and Alice and Maisie carried the tea and sandwiches up to the drawing room.

"Oh! There you are at last! I feel quite

dreadfully faint again. It's too cold in here. You must light the fire," Miss Sidebotham commanded in a feeble voice.

Maisie shook her head disgustedly, noticing that she was quite well enough to wolf down the sandwiches. "We aren't doing any more tea after this," she said sternly. "I'll light the fire, but then we have to finish getting the lunch. You'll have to put more coal on yourself." She went over to the fireplace, ignoring Miss Sidebotham's shocked mutterings about her manners and knelt down to light the fire. The maids had

 left it laid with kindling – she only needed to set a match to it and add a little coal.

"There," she said, standing up and then she coughed a little.

"Oh! It's smoking terribly, you can't have lit it properly, you silly girl!" snapped Miss Sidebotham.

Maisie felt like telling her to do it herself, but the fire *was* smoking, which was odd, as she was very used to lighting fires at home. The sweetish blue-grey smoke wafted out of the fireplace, swirling around the room and setting them all coughing. Maisie had a go at it with the poker, but it only seemed to make it worse. "Open a window," she called to Alice, but Alice was standing transfixed in the middle of the room.

"Maisie, look!" she whispered in horror. Maisie turned round from the fireplace to see the ghost cat trotting towards her, its green eyes shining through the veils of smoke.

Eddie growled and the fur rose up on the back of his neck. He stepped towards the ghost, but it ignored him, turning away from the fire and walking towards the corner of the room. Its glimmering white tail wafted from side to side and it brushed across Maisie's hand as it padded past. Then it went on through the wisps of smoke and disappeared. Maisie shivered in horror.

"It's a sign!" wailed Miss Sidebotham. "We're not long for this world. We're all cursed!"

"Oh, Maisie, it touched you," Alice whispered, her blue eyes round and frightened.

"I know…" Maisie said, staring down at her hand.

"Did it hurt you?" Alice gasped, hurrying over to look. "Has it burned you, or something awful like that?"

"No." Maisie shook her head. Now she thought about it, it hadn't hurt her at all. And it hadn't been hot, or icy, or even damp. It had felt just like any other cat – soft and warm and furry. Maisie had a feeling it wasn't a ghost at all!

Chapter Six

"It's just a cat!" Maisie told Alice again. "It seemed quite friendly to me. It's probably lived here for ages."

"Yes, hundreds of years!" Alice said, nodding her head stubbornly. "No one mentioned a cat when we arrived. If there was a cat in the house, wouldn't someone have had to feed it? It would come into the kitchens to be fed. When we said that we'd seen a white cat it wouldn't have frightened away Annie and the others, would it? They'd have told us not to be silly and that it was only the kitchen cat!"

"I suppose so," Maisie murmured. They were walking around the gardens, exercising Eddie, while Miss Sidebotham had a rest on the sofa. Maisie thought she was probably sleeping off lunch. Mrs James had prepared plenty and somehow the encounter with the not-a-ghost-cat had left everyone feeling very hungry. "Actually, I bet it smelled Miss Sidebotham's sandwiches!" she said suddenly. "Cats love fish, don't they? I should think anchovy paste sandwiches would be a real treat. Perhaps it just lives on mice. It looked ever so thin, poor thing."

"Well, whoever heard of a fat ghost?"

Alice said, throwing a stick for Eddie, so he raced off across the grass, barking excitedly. He wasn't used to such nice places to play in. Playing with him had reddened Alice's cheeks, too, and brightened her eyes. She looked worlds better. And not as worried about the phantom cat, either, now that Maisie had touched it and lived to tell the tale.

"I suppose it could be a friendly ghost," Alice said thoughtfully. "It hasn't done anything awful…"

"Actually, it's done you a favour," Maisie pointed out. "Miss Sidebotham's far too upset about being haunted to think about lessons now."

Alice laughed. "You're right, I hadn't thought of that. It's fun staying here and looking after ourselves, Maisie. If she writes a letter to Papa, I think we should – er – lose it…"

"Alice Honoria Lacey!" Maisie said, grinning. "Miss Sidebotham's right. I *am* a bad influence on you."

"Maisie, have you seen my silver bracelet?" Alice asked worriedly, coming into Maisie's

room as they were getting ready for bed
that night.

"What, the pretty one you always wear,
with the little sparkly flowers?" Maisie asked.

"Yes, I can't find it – I took it off because
I thought it would get in the way with the
cooking and the washing up. I'm sure I put it
on the kitchen windowsill, but I just went
back downstairs to fetch it and it's gone."

Maisie shook her head. "No, I haven't
seen it anywhere. You're really sure you left
it there?"

"Definitely." Alice looked at Maisie,
frowning anxiously. "Do you think it's
another ghost? Miss Sidebotham would say
it was one of the servants, but it can't have
been. I definitely had it on until lunchtime
and they'd all left by then."

Maisie snorted. "Or she'd say it was me."

"Yes, but I know it wasn't you." Alice nibbled one of her nails. "So it must have been a ghost…"

"Why would a ghost want your bracelet?" Maisie asked, but even she felt a little worried. Miss Sidebotham's spectacles still hadn't turned up and now the bracelet had disappeared as well. There was definitely something odd going on. "I don't think ghosts steal things," she said, trying to sound as though she believed it.

"But there's no one else here!" Alice glanced nervously from side to side, as though she expected ghosts to come creeping out from behind the curtains. "I'm not sure I can stay here after all, Maisie… It must be another ghost. Who knows how many of them there are?"

Maisie sighed. "Well, Miss Sidebotham

said she was going to write to your father. She told me I have to take the letter into the village tomorrow to post it."

Alice sighed. "I just don't know what to do – I do like it here, but I keep thinking something awful's going to happen…"

The next morning, Maisie hurried down the driveway with Miss Sidebotham's letter in her hand and Eddie trotting beside her. She and Alice had talked it over and decided that they ought to post the letter. Neither the bracelet nor the spectacles had turned up and the dreadful smell from the library side of the house seemed to be getting stronger.

Miss Sidebotham's letter told Mr Lacey that the house was mostly definitely haunted and probably built on the site of some

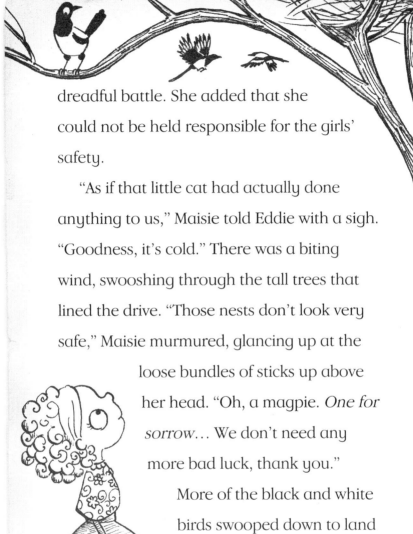

dreadful battle. She added that she could not be held responsible for the girls' safety.

"As if that little cat had actually done anything to us," Maisie told Eddie with a sigh. "Goodness, it's cold." There was a biting wind, swooshing through the tall trees that lined the drive. "Those nests don't look very safe," Maisie murmured, glancing up at the loose bundles of sticks up above her head. "Oh, a magpie. *One for sorrow…* We don't need any more bad luck, thank you."

More of the black and white birds swooped down to land in the trees, chattering and squawking, and Maisie sighed happily.

It was only a silly rhyme, of course, but still…

"There's lots of them, that's all right. *Seven for a secret, never to be told…* I wonder what it is."

She hurried on down the drive and turned into the road that ran through the village. Only a few minutes later, she could see the church spire up above her and she came into the main village street.

Maisie looked around, wondering where the post box would be. She was just deciding that she would have to ask someone – there was a cluster of people standing outside the greengrocer's shop – when one of the women walked over to her.

"Good morning, Miss."

"Oh! Hello, Annie. I didn't recognize you for a minute." The maid looked very different in her neat dark coat and a smart hat instead of her uniform.

"How are you, Miss? Have you and Miss Alice seen any more ghosts?"

Maisie looked at her carefully, trying to work out if she was serious or not. Her voice sounded as though she was really most anxious to know, but there was a hint of a smirk at the corner of her mouth.

"No… Well, we did see the ghost cat again. And the smell is getting worse…" she admitted. She didn't feel like mentioning the bracelet. Annie had been so cross with Miss Sidebotham about her spectacles and Maisie didn't want to offend her.

"Oh dear…" Annie was definitely trying not to smile, Maisie was sure of it. She thought it was funny! "I do hope that Miss Sidebotham isn't too upset about it all," Annie cooed sweetly.

"Could you tell me where to find the post box, please?" Maisie asked, trying not to sound too cross.

"Just over there, Miss," Annie said pointing. "Important letter home, is it?" She peered at the address on the letter in Maisie's hand. "To Miss Alice's father?"

"Yes." Maisie scowled. "Miss Sidebotham has written to tell him about the strange goings-on in the house."

"Oh, is that so?" Annie was smiling widely and Maisie stalked away to the post box without saying goodbye. She was sure now that Annie hadn't believed in the ghost at all. She had probably been angry that Miss Sidebotham had accused her of stealing and then had convinced everyone the ghost story was true, just to pay the governess back!

Maisie marched back to Wisteria Lodge with a determined look on her face. She was certain now that the ghosts were just a bunch of silly stories. And she was going to prove it.

Unfortunately, she had absolutely no idea how...

"How dare she?" Alice squeaked, after Maisie told her about the meeting with Annie. She banged her hands crossly into the bread dough she was kneading. "Oh, Maisie, you shouldn't have posted that letter! Now Papa will make us come home, for no reason at all."

"I know," Maisie agreed. "I almost didn't post it, but then I thought about the smell. I can't think what's causing it, but I bet it isn't good for you. And there are those shrieking noises – when I woke up this morning, I'd been dreaming that there was a ghost screaming in my ear. I jumped out of bed and then I saw that Eddie was awake too, whining, and the fur on the back of his neck was sticking up. I think there really *was* a strange noise, even if it wasn't a ghost. I heard it while I was asleep and it went into my dream. So I want to find out what it is. Besides, if we solve the mystery, we can write again and tell your father we can stay, can't we?"

"You should have woken me up and told me!" Alice said. "I'm always moaning to you about things. Urrgh. This means we have to go back to the library," she added, shuddering. "Even though I'm almost sure the ghosts were all made up, I still don't want to. It's so spooky in there."

"You don't have to come—" Maisie started to say, but Alice glared at her.

"Of course I'm coming with you! Me and Eddie are your faithful assistants." She pulled off her apron and looked rather doubtfully at the bread dough. "Do you think that looks right? It's ever such an odd greyish colour."

Maisie thought it looked dreadful, but she decided not to say so. "I'm sure it always looks like that before it's baked."

"Maybe… Come on then!" Alice started to walk bravely out of the kitchen, but she turned back before she reached the door to grab Maisie's hand.

The smell got worse and worse as they started down the passage from the entrance hall to the library. It was almost choking and the darkness of the passage made it seem even harder to breathe. They had brought a candle with them from the kitchen, but it didn't seem to burn very brightly.

"It's dreadful!" Maisie coughed, pulling out her handkerchief and pressing it to her nose as they reached the open library door.

"Are there any green mists rising out of the floor?" Alice asked, as they peered into the dim room.

"Not that I can see…" Maisie told her. "Oh, Eddie, come back!"

The little dog had pricked up his ears and then dashed into the room, barking loudly.

"It's the phantom cat!" Alice clutched Maisie's arm. "Look, there it is, walking along the back of the sofa! Eddie, don't chase it, it might do something awful to you!"

"Eddie!" Maisie yelled, but he was far too excited to listen. He never did listen when he

was chasing cats, she remembered, thinking
of that time on the way to Alice's house, a
few days before.

The ghost cat saw Eddie hurtling towards
it. It took a flying leap off the sofa and
disappeared behind one of the huge
bookcases that stuck out into the room.
Eddie went after it.

Maisie forgot the awfulness of the smell and ran after them. *That* was no ghost! Surely a ghost cat wouldn't need to run away? If Eddie tried to catch a ghost cat, he'd just run straight through it, wouldn't he? And a ghost cat wouldn't smell like a proper cat either, so Eddie probably wouldn't want to chase it anyway.

I should have thought of that before, Maisie told herself crossly. *He's behaving just like he did with that cat in the street.* It was a real cat, this proved it for sure.

She hurried round the bookcase, expecting to find Eddie and the cat hissing and scratching at each other, or maybe the cat halfway up the long velvet curtains that were draped behind the bookcase. Then she stopped in surprise and Alice caught up with her. Eddie and the cat had completely disappeared.

"Where is he?" Alice asked, and then she gave a horrified gasp. "Oh, Maisie, that ghost cat's eaten Eddie!"

"It can't have done," Maisie murmured, running her fingers along the bookcase and frowning. "Eddie didn't think that cat was a ghost and neither do I. They've just gone – somewhere."

There was a scuttling, scratching noise from behind the bookshelf and both girls took a step back, clutching each other's hands. A black nose appeared round the edge of the bookcase and Alice took in a panicked breath. Then Eddie came out into the library, looking grumpy.

"Eddie!" Both girls rushed to hug him, but even that didn't seem to cheer him up. His ears had gone back to being flat and floppy again and his eyes were gloomy. "Did that cat get away, Eddie?" Maisie said, patting him. "You shouldn't chase them, anyway. But where did you go?" She stood up and went to look round the edge of the bookcase, pushing the curtain out of the way.

A narrow, dark gap opened out behind the bookcase – just big enough for a slim person to slip through.

"Alice! Look! A secret passage!" Maisie poked her head in, holding up the candle so she could look around. "It must lead to the floor above, there's a little staircase. So this is how that white cat kept appearing and disappearing all over the place! There must be passages like this all over the house!"

Alice shuddered. "Ooohh. I don't like the sound of that – people could creep up on us all the time."

"I suppose so," Maisie agreed. "But it's very clever. I'm going to see where it goes."

Alice gulped, but she and Eddie followed Maisie into the black gap and up the winding wooden stairs.

Chapter Seven

The stairway grew lighter as they went further up and the awful smell cleared away too. "We must be getting up towards the first floor," Maisie whispered back to Alice. "There aren't any shutters over the windows up here, so that's why it's lighter. I wonder where the passage comes out?"

"I hope it's soon," Alice whispered. "There

are spiders' webs everywhere. I keep thinking I can feel little legs in my hair."

Maisie stopped suddenly, as she reached a flat wooden panel, with only a narrow strip of light down the side – just wide enough for a very thin cat to push its way through.

Eddie sniffed at it excitedly and as Maisie held the candle closer, she could see white hairs caught on the side of the panel. She hooked her fingers round it and pushed. The wooden panel creaked and stuck, then slid further across, leaving a narrow doorway.

"Look, it's my bedroom!" Maisie gasped, as she pushed the panel aside. "We've come out just behind that massive wardrobe!"

They stepped out into the room and Maisie looked back at the door, trying to work out how she'd missed a secret doorway in her own bedroom. She blew out the candle and set it down by her bed, then she went to investigate.

"Oh! You can't see the opening unless the door's pulled across all the way," she said, pulling at the sliding panel. "When it was only open enough for the cat to get through the open part was still behind the wardrobe."

"And the cat could squeeze out under the bottom of the wardrobe, I suppose," Alice agreed. "Oh, look, it's still here!"

The white cat was in the doorway between Maisie's room and Alice's, looking back at them curiously. But as soon as it spotted Eddie again, it darted away.

"Let's follow it!" Maisie said, dashing across the room with Eddie. "I want to see if there are any more secret passages. I bet that cat knows them all!"

The cat whisked round the door and into

the passage that led one way to the stairs and the other way to the warren of empty bedrooms that the girls hadn't had time to explore properly. The white cat flitted through a half-open door and Eddie and Maisie and Alice piled after it.

The room had pretty pale pink wallpaper, printed with little flowers. The curtains tied back on the four-poster bed were pink to match. It reminded Maisie of Alice's bedroom back in London.

Eddie raced across the dusty wooden floor after the cat, but for the first time it stood its ground instead of running away from him. It stopped in front of the big wooden wardrobe that stood in the corner of the room, arched its back and hissed.

Maisie and Alice stopped in surprise. Even Eddie skidded to a halt and stared at it. In his experience, cats ran – they didn't fight back.

The cat's whiskers were bristling and its green eyes were slitted and furious.

Eddie glanced uncertainly round at Maisie, then took a step towards the wardrobe.

The cat shot out a paw and raked its claws across Eddie's nose.

He whimpered and scuttled back to Maisie, with three red, oozing lines across his nose. The cat jumped through the half-open door of the wardrobe.

"Maybe there's another secret passage in there," Maisie said doubtfully. She couldn't work out why the cat had suddenly been so angry. It hadn't tried to attack Eddie until they came into this particular room.

"No, listen…" Alice edged towards the wardrobe, her eyes shining with excitement. "Can't you hear?"

Maisie followed her, with Eddie squashed worriedly up against her boots. "What is it? I can hear something squeaking, I think… Oh, has it caught a mouse?"

"No, silly!" Alice peeped inside. "Kittens!" She crouched down. "Oh, aren't they beautiful… Aren't you a clever cat!"

"They're not ghost kittens, then?" Maisie asked her, grinning, but Alice wasn't listening. She was too busy whispering endearments to the two kittens and their mother. The white cat looked at Alice suspiciously over her babies, but she seemed to understand that this girl didn't mean them any harm.

Eddie whined crossly. He didn't see why all this attention was being paid to the white cat, when it had meanly scratched him. Maisie picked him up and rubbed his ears comfortingly. "I know, it isn't fair, is it? But she must have thought you were going to hurt her kittens." She carried Eddie over to an armchair by the window and curled up on top of the dustsheet to cuddle him.

"We've solved our ghost mystery, Eddie," she murmured. "Some of it, anyway. A white cat hiding up here doesn't explain the graveyard smell. Or the shrieking noises Cissie and Lily said they heard in the library. I don't think they were lying, like Annie was. They really did look scared. And I'm sure I did hear something this morning. It was all mixed up in my dream, though. This is such a strange house. I just don't know what's real…"

Maisie gazed out of the window, trying to think what the explanation could be. She refused to believe in ghosts and graveyards, but the smell was definitely getting worse. She could even get a little hint of it all the way up here. Maybe she should open the window and let some fresh air in?

Maisie knelt up on the armchair and pulled at the window catch. It was very stiff and the window seemed to be stuck. She tried giving it a shove and then noticed that

there was a wodge of folded paper stuck into the side of the frame, holding it shut. It must have been rattling.

Maisie yanked the paper out and the window opened jerkily. She sat down again, cuddling Eddie for warmth – the fresh air was nice, but the room was chilly. She'd have to shut the window when they went back downstairs, or the kittens would freeze.

Alice was still sitting in front of the wardrobe, telling the white cat how clever she was and how beautiful her kittens were.

"Maisie, is there any fish in the larder?" she asked hopefully, looking round. "This poor cat is so thin and her kittens are getting quite big. She needs feeding up and they must need proper food too, I think."

"Miss Sidebotham's eaten all the anchovy paste. But I think there were some kippers," Maisie said. "Do cats like kippers?"

"Oh, I'm sure they do!"

Maisie sighed. She hated kippers – but perhaps the kipper whiff would hide the awful smell from the library. "I'll go and cook them, then, shall I?"

Alice beamed at her. "Would you really? Thank you, Maisie!"

Maisie wandered back down the stairs to the kitchen. She shushed Eddie and crept carefully past the drawing-room door so as not to be ambushed by Miss Sidebotham and ordered to make more sandwiches. It would be tricky anyway, as she wasn't at all convinced by Alice's breadmaking.

Maisie got the kippers out of the larder – nasty, leathery, bony things, they were. The cat was welcome to them. She went to look at the stove – Alice had let it die down a bit, she wasn't used to having to look after a fire. Maisie added some more coal and looked at it hopefully. She needed it to burn up, to get it hot enough to boil the water for jugging the kippers. If only they had some newspaper, she could put it over the front of the grate to get the fire to draw up. Maisie looked around the kitchen, but she couldn't see any – and then she remembered the wodge of paper from the window. She pulled it out of her pocket and started to unfold it, then sighed. It wasn't newspaper, it was an old letter and the sheets of paper were far too small to lay over the bars of the grate. Maisie was just about to throw the paper on the fire, when a few words caught her eye.

dreadful smell, really quite choking

Maisie wasn't sure if it was right to read other people's letters, but she was a detective after all. She wasn't just being nosy. She opened the letter out properly and frowned at the spiky writing. It made her think that the person who wrote the letter had been cross, stabbing the pen at the paper and leaving blots here and there.

We have been let this house under false pretences and I wish to complain most strongly. Clearly there is something wrong with the drains and the cesspit is blocked. I only hope that we shall not all succumb to some infectious disease. Wisteria Lodge should never have been let in this state. It is a most dreadful smell, really quite choking. We shall be leaving today and I require the return of our rent, at once.

The drains! Of course! Maisie nodded to herself. This must have been a letter to the house agent, from one of the last people to rent the house. Perhaps the letter writer had made a neater copy afterwards. This one was very hard to read, with lots of angry crossings out and blots all over it.

How could they have been so stupid? It was all that boy's fault, filling their heads with ghosts before they even got to the house. They had never thought of the simple explanation for the terrible smell, or the phantom cat.

Maisie folded her arms, frowning. That only left the shrieking noises and the strange disappearance of Alice's bracelet and Miss Sidebotham's spectacles. It was time to solve the last part of the mystery.

Chapter Eight

"Maisie! Maisie!"

"Sorry I took so long!" Maisie hurried up the rest of the stairs to Alice. "I've brought some kipper, but the cat's going to have to eat round the bones, I'm dreadful at getting them out. Oh, whatever's the matter?" Maisie stopped as she saw her friend shaking on the landing.

"Maisie, didn't you hear it?"

"No." Maisie stared at her. "No, I didn't hear a thing. What was it?"

"Screams! The most awful screams! Like you heard this morning, Maisie. They were like a soul in torment! Maybe Annie was right about the graveyard, after all."

"She wasn't," Maisie said firmly. "I've just found a letter complaining about the state of the drains. That's all the smell is. Drains. Or lack of them, I suppose. There must be an explanation for the noises, too."

"Oh… Do you think so?" Alice asked. Maisie wondered if she had been enjoying being scared, just a little. She sounded a bit disappointed that Maisie was so matter-of-fact.

"Yes. Where did they come from? Oh, here, you'd better give this to the cat,

Eddie's desperate for it." She handed a rather pretty china plate full of kipper to Alice. Eddie's tail drooped sadly.

"Oh, she'll be so pleased!" Alice glanced up. "Must we really go and look for whatever made that noise? I think it was in the attics. It definitely came from above me."

"The attic stairs are along here, I think," Maisie said. "Past the cat's room. You give her the fish, then we'll go and look upstairs."

Alice gulped and darted off to put the plate down in front of the wardrobe. Maisie held on to Eddie, who whined pitifully, as though no one had ever given him so much as a whitebait.

"Sssshhh," Maisie told him. "I'll give you something much, much nicer when we've found out what's making those noises. You did help us solve our ghost mystery, after all."

Alice tiptoed reluctantly back into the passage and when Maisie opened the door up to the servants' rooms and the attic stairs, she shuddered. "I suppose we must…" she whispered, as she followed Maisie.

The attic floor was enormous, much larger than the attics back at Maisie's house in London. They were full of broken furniture, dusty old paintings and trunks packed with old clothes. Maisie would have liked to explore properly, and Alice cried out with delight at a box full of old hats, trailing faded feathers and wisps of net.

"We can look later," Maisie said firmly. "We have to find where the noise came from, first. Maybe it was just a creaking door, blowing in the wind?"

"It was not a door, Maisie," Alice said firmly. "You wouldn't say that if you'd heard it. And why would the doors creak, anyway? The windows up here aren't open."

"Hmmm. I suppose not… It *is* chilly, though." Maisie shivered. "Maybe the draught comes down the chimney."

Just then, the most unearthly shrieking noise echoed around the room, a shrill wail that stopped Maisie's breath and made her and Alice clutch at each other in panic.

"Let's go! Let's go!" Alice whimpered, and even Eddie cowered against the two girls as though he thought something awful was coming after them all.

"Wait!" Maisie gasped. "I don't believe in ghosts! I don't!" she muttered to herself. Although it was very hard to be sure, with the echoes of that dreadful shriek still in her ears. "There's been an explanation for the other things," she whispered shakily. "There must be an explanation for this, too." She took a step towards the fireplace. "Did you think it came from over there?"

"Maybe," Alice agreed, but she didn't follow Maisie. "It seemed to go all round the room. Like a ghost was flying around us."

"I think it was from the fireplace," Maisie muttered. Digging her nails into her palms, she crept over towards the little grate and looked at it curiously. It was full of sticks, as though someone had been trying to light a fire. "Ghosts don't need fires," she told herself firmly and leaned further in to peer up the chimney.

Another terrible scream echoed down and Maisie screamed back, stumbling and slipping on to her side. There was a strange chattering noise and a squawking and another pile of sticks and soot fell into the grate.

Maisie stared at it and then wriggled closer and looked up the chimney again. Then she coughed as another cloud of soot collapsed down the chimney and left black smuts all over her face.

"What is it?" Alice gasped. "Come away from it, Maisie!"

"It's magpies!" Maisie began to laugh. "Oh, Alice, that's all it is! A flock of magpies! I saw them in the big trees on the drive when I went down to the village and they were screeching like anything, but I never thought about it. They must have made nests on top of the other chimneys too, that's why the fires don't draw properly!" She leaned forward suddenly and dug about among the sticks in the fireplace.

"And look! Your bracelet, Alice! And Miss Sidebotham's spectacles. And one, two, three, four silver spoons!"

"How on earth did all that get there?" Alice demanded, running forward. She snatched up her bracelet and slipped it back on to her wrist with a grateful smile.

"Professor Tobin told me a story about a magpie once," Maisie said, running the gold chain through her fingers as she tried to remember. "There was a girl who was accused of stealing, but it turned out it was a magpie all along. They like shiny things and they hide them in their nests." She giggled. "I saw seven of them, I remember now. *Seven for a secret, never to be told.* But we found their secret after all!"

"There's a carriage coming down the drive!" Maisie reported to Alice the next morning, as they were playing with the kittens. The bread had looked rather flat and strange after it had been baked, but it had tasted nice and they had made toast for breakfast. Miss Sidebotham complained bitterly that there wasn't anything more substantial, but she still wouldn't even think of descending to the kitchens to help. And she had been grateful for the return of her spectacles, although the first thing she did was to put them on and tell Maisie off for letting the drawing room get so disgracefully dusty.

Alice got up carefully, cradling a white kitten against her shoulder as she came to look out of the bedroom window. "Do you think it's Papa coming to fetch us?" she asked excitedly. "I shall ask if we can take the dear cat and her kittens home with us. We can't possibly leave them here all on their own. I'm going to name the mother Snowflake, but I haven't decided on names for the kittens yet. You'll have to help me, Maisie. We can make a list. It will be a good way to keep ourselves busy on the journey home."

"I don't think Miss Sidebotham likes cats," Maisie warned her, but Alice's eyes flashed.

"I don't care! I shall tell Papa just how useless she has been and how you've had to do all the work. Oh, yes, it was mostly you, Maisie, I only helped a little." She smiled. "I shall put on my best darling daughter face and cough a little and Papa will let me have a hundred cats if I like." Then she sighed. "But I shall miss being here with you, Maisie. It will be terribly boring back in London, even if I've got the kittens to play with."

"I know." Maisie nodded, although the thought of going back to London and seeing Gran and Sally and Professor Tobin was like a warm glow inside her. "Perhaps you could ask for extra French lessons with Madame Lorimer and then we might have more of a chance to talk?"

Alice shook her head firmly. "Oh no. I'm going to ask Papa if you can visit us properly now, without us having to hide from Miss Sidebotham all the time. Although we might have to leave Eddie in the kitchens – I don't think he will ever get on with my darling Snowflake."

They hurried down the stairs to open the front door to Mr Lacey, each clutching a kitten, with Snowflake and Eddie jumping from step to step, hissing and yapping at each other. Maisie smiled to herself. She had a feeling that Alice was going to get exactly what she wanted. And it really had been the most exciting mystery. She must remember to tell the professor about the magpies, and she was sure that Gran and Sally would be spellbound by the tale of the ghosts that never were…

Activities

Test your detective skills and knowledge with these activities, and learn more about Victorian ghosts!

Find the answers on pages 166–168!

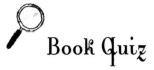

Book Quiz

Now you've read the book, have a go at answering the questions below! You may need to look back over the story to help you.

1. What disgusting dish does Alice say she will throw on the fire if she's served it?

2. How does Mary-Ann the maid hide Eddie from the butler?

3. How many dolls are on the mantelpiece in Alice's bedroom?

4. What does Alice's father smoke?

5. What kind of a train do Maisie, Alice and Miss Sidebotham board to get to the country?

6. What does Miss Sidebotham find is missing at breakfast time?

7. Why does Maisie walk to the village?

8. What do the girls find behind the library bookcase?

9. What does Maisie feed the cat?

10. Who has been stealing the jewellery and other valuable things?

Spot the Difference

Detectives need to be very observant to spot clues. Can you see five differences in the second picture opposite?

159

Victorian Ghost Stories

The Victorians loved their ghost stories, and were thrilled by all things mysterious and occult. Many places in Britain still have myths surrounding them of hauntings and strange goings-on. Maisie doesn't believe in ghosts, but she might have enjoyed reading some of these spooky Victorian stories…

A Christmas Carol by Charles Dickens
First published: 1843

This much-loved tale follows the miserly Ebeneezer Scrooge who employs Bob Cratchit as a clerk. He pays very low wages, so he's grown wealthy as the Cratchits have become desperately poor. On Christmas Eve, Scrooge goes to bed, but is woken by the ghost of his old business partner Jacob Marley. Marley is a terrifying sight to behold, and he warns Scrooge to change his ways or face an afterlife of misery. Then follows three ghosts, who each take Scrooge on a journey. The Ghost of Christmas Past shows Scrooge himself as a boy, and The Ghost of Christmas Present reveals the home of the Cratchits as they prepare for a merry but pitiful Christmas feast. Scrooge discovers that the youngest son, Tiny Tim, is very ill, but the Cratchits can't afford medicine. The Ghost of Christmas Yet To Come shows Scrooge the result of his cruelty: Tiny Tim will die. Scrooge sees his own grave – which has never been visited. He awakes on Christmas morning, and rejoices to find he is alive. Grateful for a second chance, he decides to be a better man – starting with sending a delicious turkey to the Cratchits.

The Canterville Ghost by Oscar Wilde
First published: 1887

This short, funny story follows the
wealthy Otis family from America as they
settle into their new home – the haunted
Canterville Chase. The ghost who lives there,
Sir Simon, hopes to frighten them from his
house: he makes horrifying sounds as he
rattles his chains and he leaves a bloodstain
on the carpet. Much to Sir Simon's
annoyance, the Otises aren't in the least bit
frightened. Mr Otis offers him some oil to
stop his chains from rattling, and the
bloodstains are cleaned up. Two of the
children play tricks on the poor ghost,
sending him flying down stairs and
drenching him with water. Nothing Sir Simon
can do will scare them, and it's only when
Virginia Otis, the daughter, helps him that
he finally finds peace at last.

The Hound of the Baskervilles
by Arthur Conan Doyle
First published: 1901-1902

This chilling novel is set on Dartmoor, where the Baskerville family are frightened by a terrible legend, which tells of an ancestor who gave his soul to the devil and was transformed into a murderous demon dog… Now, Sir Charles Baskerville has unexpectedly been found dead from a heart attack, with animal footprints by his body. The famous detective Sherlock Holmes is brought in to solve the mystery.

Eventually, Holmes deduces that Sir Charles died after being chased by a huge dog made to look like a hellhound – the culprit covered it in phosphorus, which glows a ghostly green. The murderer was a disgraced nephew of Sir Charles, out to trick his way to his inheritance, but he falls to his doom on the moor.

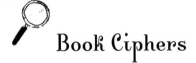

Book Ciphers

One of the things a detective might have to do is crack a code, to figure out messages sent between criminal gangs, or to help solve a puzzling crime.

Codes work by scrambling messages so they appear to be nonsense to someone stumbling across them. To read a coded message, you need to have the key, which is like a solution.

Maisie and Alice tried making up their own code, using *Oliver Twist* as a key. This is called a book cipher, and the messenger and the recipient each need a copy of the same book, the key, for it to work.

Below is a message, written using this book as a key. You can read it like this:
8, 10, 7 = Page 8, line 10, 7th word = treacle

Now try this message:

8, 10, 7. 22, 19, 1. 60, 10, 6.
93, 18, 4. 58, 13, 5. 21, 18, 1!

And here is a longer one:

19, 19, 7. 117, 2, 5. 151, 8, 7.
10, 1, 3. 26, 19, 2. 64, 5, 7.
8, 12, 5. 113, 9, 5.

18, 2, 5. 30, 17, 5. 150, 13, 4.
14, 19, 2. 63, 4, 5. 66, 2, 7.
141, 12, 2. 8, 19, 1. 149, 19, 1!

Now you've got the hang of it, why not try writing your own cipher and sending messages to your best friend? Just make sure she has the same book as you, and keep it secret!

Answers

Page 156 – Book Quiz:

1. Calves' foot jelly! This yucky-sounding food was made by boiling calves' feet and was thought to be good for invalids in Victorian times.

2. By hiding him in the laundry basket! In those days, washing clothes was exhausting. The maids had to boil clothes in a pot, scrub them with such things as milk, chalk or onion juice, and then turn them through a mangle to squeeze out the water.

3. Three dolls, plus one teddy bear! Alice's dolls would have been much more delicate than modern toys. They often had wool hair and porcelain faces, so care had to be taken when playing with them!

4. A pipe. Victorian gentlemen liked to make a ritual out of smoking tobacco. They wore special velvet jackets and retired to another room after dinner so as not to upset the ladies!

5. A steam train. In the cabin, there would have been a fireman shovelling coal into the firebox, which heated water into steam and turned the engine. Hot, tiring and very dirty!

6. Her pince-nez spectacles. "Pince-nez" means "nose-pincher" and they were a popular style at the time. They even feature in a Sherlock Holmes story, "The Adventure of the Golden Pince-Nez".

7. To post a letter to Alice's father. The postal service was reformed during the Victorian times so that people paid in advance to send a letter using the first "Penny Black" stamps, which cost one pence!

8. A secret passageway and a staircase. Grand houses often had small servants' staircases running between floors, so the owners didn't have to see their servants going about their business!

9. Kippers. These are whole smoked herrings, and they were very popular as a breakfast dish until the early twentieth century.

10. The magpies! These intelligent birds are related to crows, and there were lots of myths about them in the past, especially because they like to steal things for their nests.

Page 158 – Spot the Difference:

Page 165 – Book Ciphers:
Message 1: Treacle pudding not calves' foot jelly!
Message 2: Next meeting will be at 31 Albion Street.
Bring your kittens and look out for Miss Sidebotham!

Coming Soon:

The Case of the Feathered Mask

Maisie's friend Professor Tobin has travelled all over the world and she loves to look at the amazing objects he's collected on his adventures. Now he plans to donate his collection to the British Museum – including the rare and valuable Feathered Mask. But when a thief breaks into the boarding house and steals the mask, leaving only a feather, Maisie realizes she has a new mystery on her hands.

Maisie Hitchins

The Case of the Stolen Sixpence

HOLLY WEBB

Have you read?

The Case of the Stolen Sixpence

When Maisie rescues an abandoned puppy, he quickly leads her to her first case. George, the butcher's boy, has been sacked for stealing, but Maisie's sure he's innocent. It's time for Maisie to put her detective skills to the test as she follows the trail of the missing money...

Have you read?

The Case of the Vanishing Emerald

When star-of-the-stage Sarah Massey comes to visit, Maisie senses a mystery. Sarah is distraught – her fiancé has given her a priceless emerald necklace and now it's gone missing. Maisie sets out to investigate, but nothing is what it seems in the theatrical world of make-believe…

For sneak peaks, fun facts, competitions and more, visit:

www.maisiehitchins.com

Maisie Hitchins

ACTIVITIES

Things
to do

READ

A sample
chapter from
the first book

win

Enter the
competition

HOLLY WEBB

About the
author

Find out more about Holly Webb

www.holly-webb.com